Who Has Time
for
Little Bear?

Who Has Time for Little Bear?

Ursel Scheffler

illustrated by Ulises Wensell

A DOUBLEDAY BOOK FOR YOUNG READERS

Little Bear woke up first. Spring was here! He ran to the front of the den. Then he woke up Papa Bear and Mama Bear. He tugged at their fur and shouted, "Wake up! The sun is shining!"

"Grrrrrr. I'm still sleepy," Papa Bear growled.

"Me too," sighed Mama Bear, and she turned over.

Little Bear danced and sang in front of the den. At last Papa Bear and Mama Bear came outside. They squinted into the light. The spring sun warmed their fur.

"I'm hungry," said Papa Bear, stretching. "My stomach is growling louder than I am."

"Achoo!" Mama Bear sneezed. "I think I'm catching a cold."

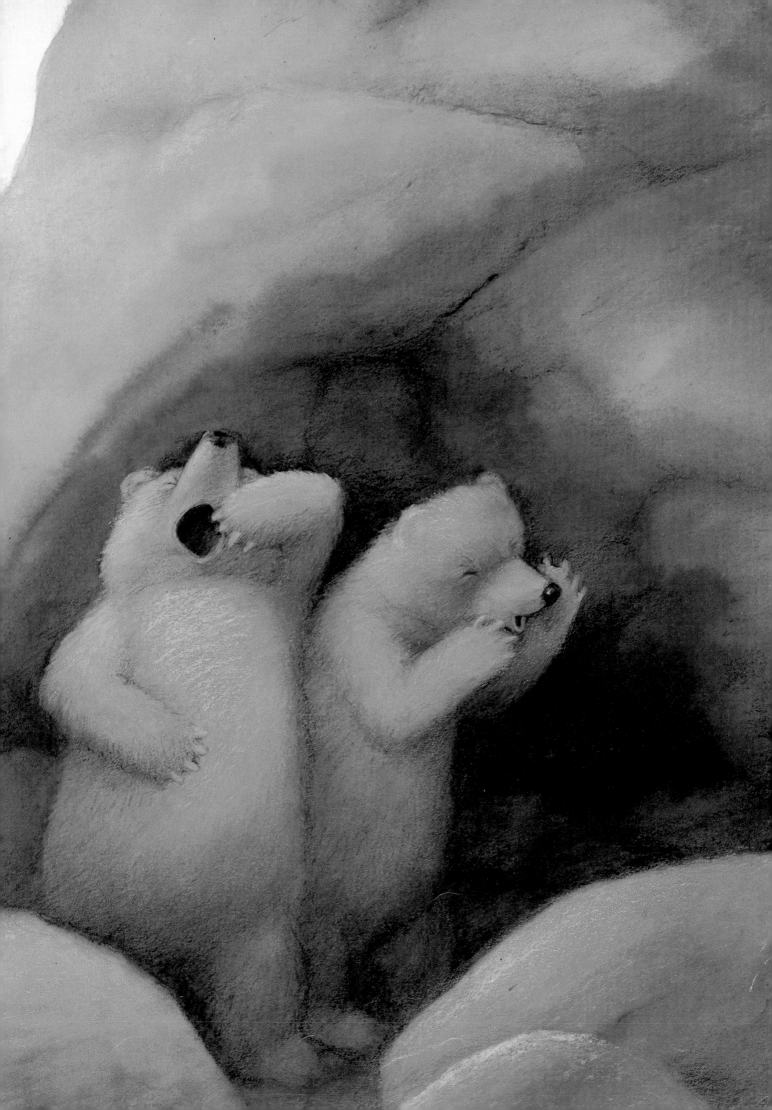

As they sat around the fire for lunch, Papa Bear said,
"No wonder your mama has the sniffles. Our den is cold
and damp. We should build a log cabin with a cozy
oven."
"That's a great idea!" said Mama Bear.

They started collecting logs right away.
"Watch out! Out of the way, so you don't get hurt!"
shouted Papa Bear.
Little Bear sprang to the side.
In no time they had built the foundation.

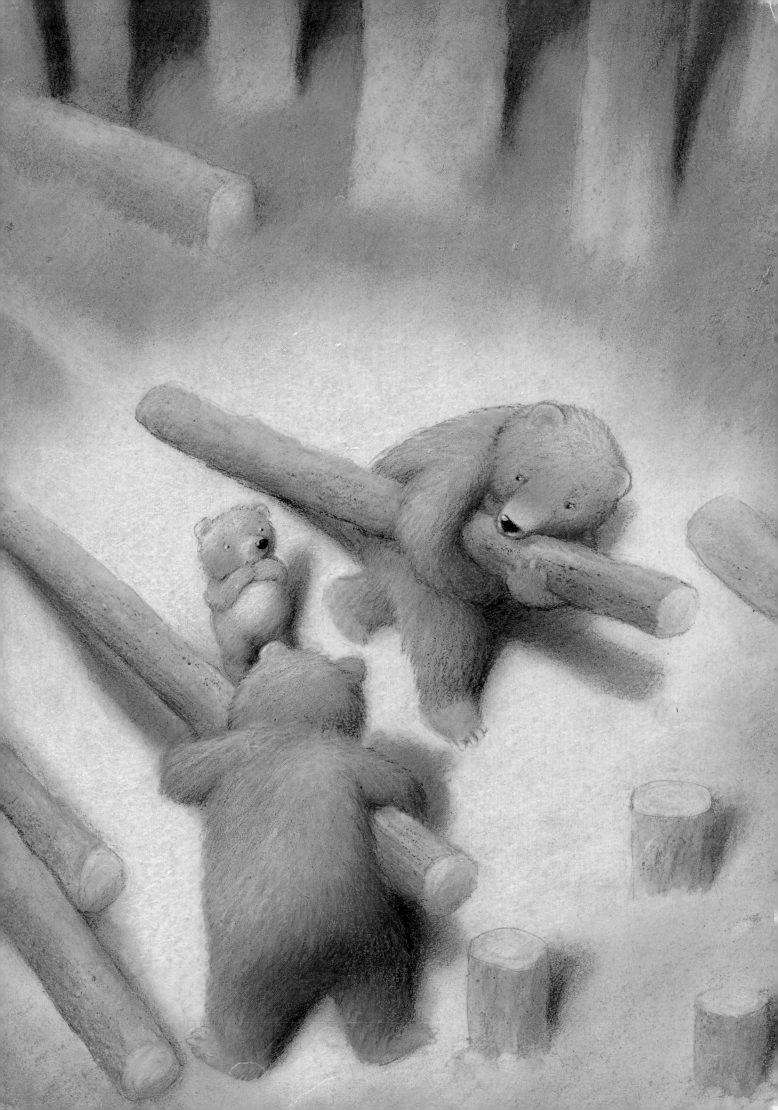

The house grew bigger and bigger. Mama Bear sawed
the logs, and Papa Bear hammered them in.

"Out of the way, so you don't fall down!" shouted
Mama Bear when Little Bear climbed on the logs. Little
Bear jumped down.

"I don't know how to help," he growled. He was getting
very bored.

"Build a house of twigs," said Mama Bear.

"With a roof of branches," said Papa Bear.

So Little Bear started to build his own house of twigs.

When his house was finished, Little Bear shouted, "Papa! Mama! Look at my house of twigs!"

"In a minute," said Papa Bear, and he kept hammering.

"Later," said Mama Bear, and she kept sawing.

They did not have time for Little Bear.

Little Bear ran into the forest. He was very unhappy.

"Somewhere there must be someone with time for me," he thought.

At the old oak Little Bear saw a woodpecker. He was pecking around his new nest.

"I built a house too. May I show it to you?" asked Little Bear.

"Sorry, but I don't have time," said the woodpecker, and he kept pecking.

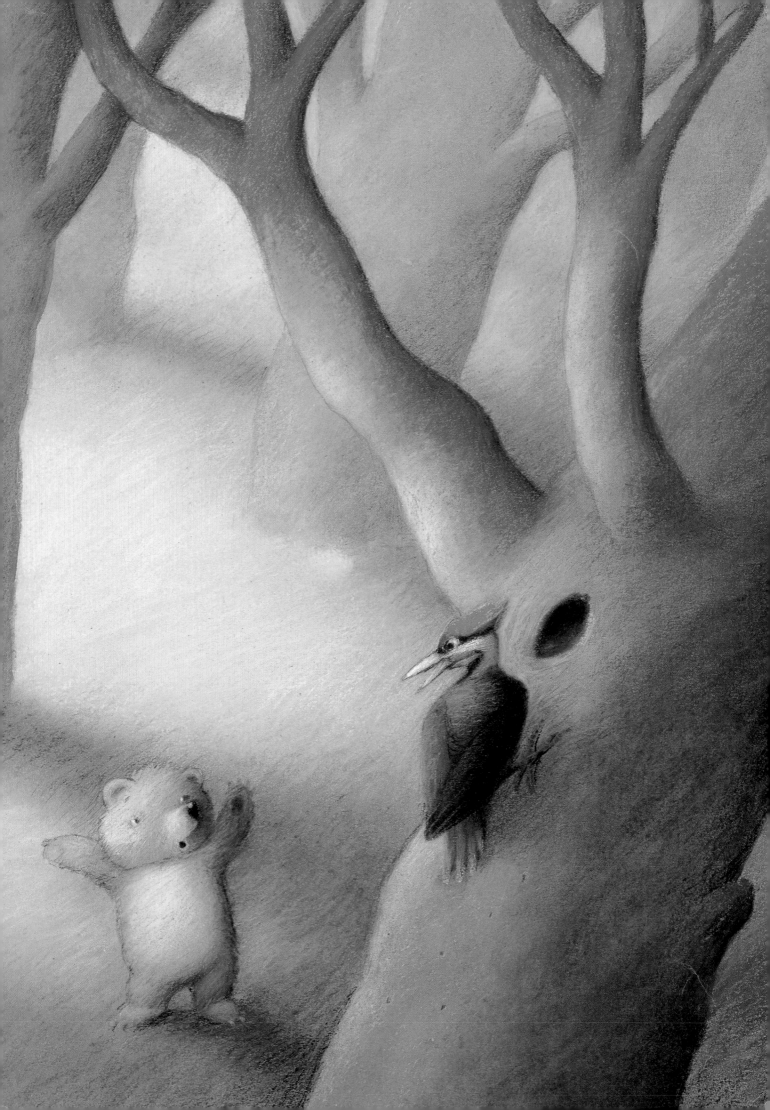

At a big rock, Little Bear met a squirrel. She was very
upset, because she had forgotten where she had hidden
the last nuts of her winter stock. At the oak? At the
beech? At the maple?

"Can I show you my house of twigs at the edge of the
forest?" asked Little Bear.

"Sorry, that's too far away. I don't have time," said the
squirrel. And she ran off through the rustling grass.

At last Little Bear came to the meadow. There he saw a mole, leaning against a rock. He seemed to have time.

"Look how hard I've worked," said the mole, and proudly pointed to the meadow. "I've built one hundred and thirty mole hills. And nobody noticed."

"That's what happened to me," said Little Bear. "May I show you my house of twigs?"

"Sorry, but my lunch break is over," said the mole, and he picked up his spade. "I have to get back to work."

Little Bear was very sad. Didn't anybody have time for him? He was so disappointed, his throat hurt. He swallowed and ran down to the river for a drink.

At the edge of the water he stopped in surprise. There was another little bear! He had just caught a salmon.

"Look, isn't it huge?" shouted the other bear.

"It's the biggest fish I ever saw!" said Little Bear, amazed.

The other bear was very proud.

The two bears made a campfire and roasted the fish.
They ate and drank and told each other stories.

"It's nice to have a little time, isn't it?" said Little Bear,
smiling.

The other bear smiled back.

"Can I be your friend?" he asked.

Little Bear thought. "You are my friend," he said. "A
friend is someone who has time for you. May I show you
my house of twigs?"

"I'd love to see it!" said Little Bear's friend.

They ran up the hill, across the meadow, and through
the woods, right to the edge of the forest.

Papa and Mama Bear had almost finished the log cabin. They'd been working so hard, they hadn't even noticed how long Little Bear had been gone. He proudly showed his new friend the house of twigs.

"It's the nicest house I ever saw!" said Little Bear's friend, amazed. "We should build a tiny backyard with a tiny swing . . ."

" . . . and a tiny fence with a tiny gate!" shouted Little Bear.

They started to work right away.

"Could you hand me that box of nails, Little Bear?" called Papa Bear from the top of the ladder.

"Sorry, I don't have time," Little Bear answered. He was just fitting the tiny gate into the tiny fence. It was really very complicated work.

"Do I have to do everything myself?" grumbled Papa Bear as he climbed down the ladder.

But the two little bears didn't notice him, they were so
busy. They were friends now, and they had time for each
other and for nothing else in the world.

A Doubleday Book for Young Readers
Published by Bantam Doubleday Dell Publishing Group, Inc.
1540 Broadway, New York, New York 10036
First American Edition 1998
Originally published in Germany by Ravensburger Buchverlag
as „Wer hat Zeit für den kleinen Bären?“
Doubleday and the portrayal of an anchor with a dolphin are trademarks of
Bantam Doubleday Dell Publishing Group, Inc.
Copyright © 1996 Ravensburger Buchverlag
Library of Congress Cataloging-in-Publication Data
ISBN: 0-385-32536-3
Cataloging-in-Publication Data is available from the U.S. Library of Congress.

The text of this book is set in 16-point Goudy • Book design by Semadar Megged
Manufactured in Germany • September 1998
10 9 8 7 6 5 4 3 2 1